RACK AND WRUIN

Rudyard Thurber

BANYAN TREE PRESS

RACK AND WRUIN

ISBN-13: 978-1-936449-08-8

LIBRARY OF CONGRESS CONTROL NUMBER: 2011933908

BANYAN TREE PRESS

WWW.BANYANTREEPRESS.COM

ENGLEWOOD, COLORADO

AUSTIN, TEXAS

COVER/INTERIOR BY: DPMediaPro.com

PRINTED IN U.S.A

Contents

Nuances 63

Needs Music

About the Author

By Way of Introduction

I have been thinking about the idea of "You can't take it with you" when it occurred to me you can.

I am what is kindly described as a senior. Seniors have a lot of untapped usefulness in them, especially things in the mind. Our life is a crazy quilt of experiences, insights, lessons, stories, etc., that, unless captured in some way will leave this earth with us. In my case, it's probably no big deal.

But, I have these scraps, these multihued bits and pieces I felt like writing down. There was no way to weave this into a coherent, contiguous document so please accept its organization as it is. I was going to call this book "The Joy of Being a Stoic" but I hate to have to explain what has already been uttered.

But, this book is also about you! If you have been wanting to share some things over the years, do it! I like a good story and so do many others. In fact, I sometimes think reading is going to be a lost art like penmanship so I feel rather obligated to change that since I personally love to read.

Anyway, I hope you enjoy some, if not all, the contents herein. Please don't be too harsh in your judgments. These are only my views, not necessarily those of management.

DEDICATION

For Terry and Angie: May God preserve what you had and, when
you're together again, may He reinstate it at full vigor.

JUST SO-SO STORIES

CLIFFDWELLER

The car went noiselessly off the road and began its plummet. Its passenger, an engineer named Hobbes, had fallen asleep at the wheel after a long day on top of the mesa known as Los Alamos. Mr. Hobbes' engineering group had come up with an important proposal for the government to consider and he was designated to be the representative of this pitch in Washington.

He had made this drive many times but, especially at night and even more especially, at night in the rain, this road would scare Jesus Himself. It was barely misting when he left the top of the mesa but had increased in intensity as he descended.

Quickly, the car made its first bump on the hillside which activated all the airbags and woke Mr. Hobbes. He, in his grogginess, had no idea where he was until the second bump.

"Oh, my God!"

The car seemed to be turning over and over as well until the third bump when it suddenly stopped moving entirely.

Mr. Hobbes took a few moments to assess, being an engineer and all.

His briefcase was in total disarray with papers all over the car. He had no idea where his cell phone was. He was belted in and, upon unbuckling, found he had very little room to operate with a bent up passenger compartment. He surmised the car was lying sideways on the driver side. The headlights pointed off into nowhere.

Using the driver side control, he tried opening the passenger side window but got pelted with rain.

He knew he was expected back in Albuquerque later this evening by his family. He had expected to spend the night at home before heading out on a flight the next morning.

Hours passed. The rain ceased. Hobbes became aware of soreness in his left shoulder. He had tried to sleep but the pain kept him awake.

As the sun arose over the Sangre de Cristo Mountains behind him, he began to formulate a survival plan. It was very limited in scope and hope as he knew his ultimate survival depended upon being found within a couple of days.

First, he tested the horn. It worked. He decided to hit it once an hour as a signal until the battery gave out.

He discovered he could move the seat back which greatly improved his comfort level as it gave him room to move around a little. Looking up he could see mountainside and trees but not the road. Twisting around a little, he could see his car was pinned between the rock face and a sturdy (he hoped) pine.

He turned on the car radio and began to search for news. He was starting to get hungry. Looking for ideas, he opened the center console. There was a little notepad, a pen, a rosary, and his cab card and insurance card. He closed the console and tried to look into the back between the bucket seats. He knew his cell phone would probably be unreachable in his current position.

He turned off the radio to save energy.

That evening it rained again. This time, he opened the passenger window and tried to drink the rainwater as best he could.

Sometime, during the second day, Mr. Hobbes decided to take out the notepad and pen and make some notes. He spent an hour or so deciding what to write and, naturally enough given the circumstances, decided to write to his family. It occurred to him he should update his will but he put it off until later.

Replacing the notepad into the console, his hand touched the rosary. He began to think about that. "I wonder if I even remember how to say the rosary anymore." He took out the rosary. "Let's see. Today is . . .

" He had no idea what day it was. He decided he would think about it for a while and put the rosary back into the console. "Odd." He thought. He only happened to have it in the car because his mother had always made him have one on him somewhere from boyhood on. He spent some time, then, thinking about his parents.

It did not rain that evening. By now, Mr. Hobbes was getting fairly hungry. He began to think about pizza before dropping off to a fitful sleep.

On the morning of the third day, Mr. Hobbes felt mostly defeated. His grizzled and whiskered face did not smile. He tried to get comfortable but only aggravated his sore shoulder. For some reason, he could only think of the rosary sitting in the console right next to him. He decided to try it. He began, as he remembered, with what he could remember of the creed and then the "Our Father." He decided to do the sorrowful mysteries given his situation.

As he got to the end of the fifth mystery, he began to think about other prayers. Prayers he had forgotten or forgotten to say over the years. He also said some ad lib prayers asking for deliverance from his predicament.

He put the rosary away and drifted off into a kind of peaceful nap. It did not rain this evening either.

The next day, almost comatose, he awoke to a glorious, sunny day. He tried the horn a few times just in case. He still had some battery left.

As he lay there, he thought about writing some more but felt too weak to try. He decided to pray some more.

This time, his ad lib prayers were prayers of thanks. Thanks for his life, his family and friends. He found himself praying for others that he knew were in need of such. He prayed the rosary again, this time the glorious mysteries. He spent some time on reflection and asked God for forgiveness for his many transgressions. He found himself softly crying.

Afterward, he put the rosary away in what was now a sacred place. He lay there thinking for a long while and then drifted off into a somber sleep half-expecting to not awaken again.

He heard breaking glass. Why was he hearing breaking glass when he was dead?

"Mr. Hobbes!" "Are you okay?"

He opened his eyes and thought he heard and saw people.

He half smiled and closed his eyes again.

"Mr. Hobbes!" "Wake up!"

It was rather insistent. Hobbes open his eyes again and, this time, studied what he saw.

"Help!" he said weakly.

"We're going to help." "You're going to be okay."

The EMT then explained that they would winch his car up to the road before extracting him. Hobbes was in no condition to argue.

———————————

Days later, the impound lot called Hobbes to ask if there was anything he wanted to retrieve from his car. If so, could he come down and get them. Without thinking he responded there wasn't but, then, had an insight. "Wait a minute. Where are you located? I might want to come down and check it out."

The car was a terrible, twisted mess. The passenger door worked but that was about all. Hobbes looked inside and spotted his briefcase. He gathered it and all the papers he could find. Then, he remembered his note. He reached into the console and, as he was pulling it out, touched the rosary again.

He placed the holy item in his pocket.

"Thanks." he said.

Pillboxed In

This is a true story. Honestly.

I recently turned sixty-four years old. Too young for Medicare Part XYZ or any of it. I did, however, get a marketing birthday card from a Prominent Twin Cities HMO suggesting I apply for their supplemental coverage. I have no health insurance coverage and, knowing the Dreaded Democratic Doctor Deputies were undoubtedly closing in on me to have me arrested, I thought I'd take the initiative so I called HMO. (Note: I have since learned HMO stands for Hand the Money Over.)

"Hello there. How may I help?"

"I need to get some insurance and you sent me a birthday card for my sixty-fourth birthday. Thank you for the card, by the way."

"No Problem. We have several plans that would fit your situation. Plan A is blah blah blah. Plan B is blah blah blah. Plan C is blah blah blah. Tell me—are you in good health?"

"No."

"No? Why not?"

"Nine years ago I had a quad bypass."

"Oh. In that case, you would qualify for none of our plans. You must call the Minnesota Comprehensive Health Association at xxx-xxxx."

"Why do I need to call them?"

"Because they exist for people like you."

I have suddenly and arbitrarily been reclassified with the ubiquitous "people like you." Side Note: We play at a lot of senior card games and there is this one woman who constantly refers to every one else as "you people." She's been a part of our group for years now which raises the question "When does she qualify to be one of "us people?"

I call MCHA.

"MCHA. How may I direct your call?"

"I need to get health insurance and I've been turned down elsewhere so they sent me to you."

"You can qualify if you've been turned down elsewhere."

"I just said I was turned down elsewhere. Where do I sign?"

"You need to send in an application with a copy of your rejection letter."

"I didn't get a rejection letter—it was a verbal rejection."

"We need a written copy of your rejection."

"All right."

Do you get the feeling I'm gaining on this? Me neither.

"Prominent Twin Cities HMO. How may I help you?"

"Yes. You people (Boy that felt good!) just rejected me for health insurance. Then you sent me to MCHA. MCHA wants a copy of the rejection letter. Can you send me a rejection letter?"

"You can't get a rejection letter unless you send in an application."

Ladies and Gentlemen—I kid you not.

The upshot of all this is that I will follow this procedure:

Apply at Prominent Twin Cities HMO

Wait for Rejection

Make copy of rejection and apply at MCHA

Obviously, we could all be dead by the time this thing is over. But, once there, the process gets much easier. All I'll have to do then is decide every month to pay for insurance or pay the rent.

TROPHIES

O n the sine curve that describes life, I have reached the
point of decumulation. What do I do with all this stuff?
After a lifetime (so far) of acquisition and finally coming to the
realization that no one is probably going to build a museum of me,
I realize either I do this or my kids will and I don't hate them that
much. In fact, I kind of like them.

The treasures of my life are, in truth, probably treasures only to me.
And I drag them from place to place, always finding a shelf of honor for
each of them in their new home.

There are books. Thousands of books. Who could possibly read
them all? Clearly I am in need of a twelve-step program for this addiction.
I have no more room for them, yet I still buy them. I have become
acquainted with the idea of storage. Now, most of these treasures lie
behind a padlock in an unheated garage-sized room on some stranger's
land. Probably never read a book in his life.

Albums. Hundreds of albums. CD's are just a passing fad, right?
And I can't even spell MP3. At least they're not eight-tracks. If I have six
hundred albums and each has twelve tracks and each track runs three
minutes, how much longer will I have to live just to hear all the songs?
How can I legitimately put that onus on one of the kids?

There are treasures of my youth. Ribbons, medals, plaques,
trophies from long-forgotten local events that may or may not have been
important enough to make the paper in which case, there may be old,
sepia-colored clippings to read. A graduation program. Hey—it's over!
Throw it away!

But, I can't. It's part of my life. The ascension of the sine curve.
What formed me. What informed me.

I suppose it all comes down to the kids, after all, throwing everything away after I'm gone and I'm not present to rue the loss of my treasures.

And the curve closes on the x axis.

BIN SITES

By the 1950s and 1960s, the U. S. farmer had achieved such a production rate without over-fertilizing or over-irrigating that the government instituted a couple of novel practices.

One was called the Soil Bank wherein farmers were paid NOT to grow certain crops and to let a portion of their farmland lie fallow for that year.

The second dealt with surplus grain by establishing bin sites outside most agricultural communities. Each town had a plot of land with some metal silo bins as well as a few of the Quonset type.

When father quit farming, he became the maintenance person for all the bin sites in Kingsbury County, South Dakota. Each day, he would take a lunch prepared by mother and head out to a different town for the day. He managed to find enough to keep him busy at each site for an entire day. I went with him one day to the town of Badger. Not a big town. I managed to walk the entire town in about fifteen minutes so I had to spend the rest of the day waiting.

(Just this week, a headline on the internet said the U. N. believes more than one billion people are now starving.)

I have to admit, farming never got into my blood. Even today, I have no desire to even grow a garden. But, father, like a true farmer, loved the soil.

I have a younger brother, almost my age, who might have learned to like farming but for a close call one day. I was in the kitchen when dad walked in holding my brother in his arms. He had been riding on the back of the tractor out to the field. Most tractors have a shaft sticking out the back of the tractor called a Power Take Off or "PTO." Usually, there is a flip down cover to lower for safety's sake. This tractor did not have that.

The PTO shaft caught on my brother's belt and started twisting. If the belt had not broke, his spine would probably have been snapped. We all carry distinct images into our old age and the vision of dad carrying him still scares me.

On the way to the doctor's office that morning, dad had the car all the way up to fifty. It was a Willys. Our fleet was a succession of them and Henry Js and Studebakers. Other kids' dads were buying the latest Pontiac or other current stock car racing giant. They got thrills. We got economy.

Another aspect of farming, of course, was livestock. We had beef cattle and milk cows of dubious lineage, some pigs, chickens and a flock of turkeys that showed up one day and mother conned them into staying. We were never short on a meat to eat, especially if you throw in the frequent pheasant.

With farm animals there is sometimes tragedy. We had this big strapping calf who was trying to get a drink from the water tank one cold winter day. Over the course of the winter, there had been an ice buildup where we would chop the ice for them to drink. As the calf walked up to the tank I had an instant vision of it slipping and falling into the tank. Then, it did just that and floated under the ice still in the tank. I wasn't big enough to do anything about it so I ran after father and by the time we got back the calf was dead. Dad had to use a block and tackle assembly to pull it out of the tank.

Getting water to the tank in the winter was a chore in itself. This is where corn cobs come in. The pipe from the windmill to the tank was plumbed for positive feed to the tank but, on severely cold days and when it was not in use for a while, the water still in the pipes would freeze. So you would hook your corn cob to a clothes hanger, soak the cob in kerosene, light it, and walk up and down the pipeline until water started to run.

There were other uses for corn cobs including heating the house and another application involving the outhouse when the catalogue was used up.

It was a wonderful and simple time. We even had our own classification system a la Myers-Briggs! There were four absolutes in those days, four choices. Republican / Democrat; Catholic / Protestant; Ford / Chevy; and (Brooklyn) Dodgers / Yankees. While we did not go to wine tasting parties and say things like "Hi, I'm Carl and I'm an ENTJ" we would eventually get to know the choices of those we were growing up with.

My best friend suffered from being on the fringe with regard to the baseball choices. He made the distressed choice of Kansas City as his ball team only to see favorite players such as Bobby Shantz, Bob Cerv, and someone named Maris all traded to the Yankees. Nothing much has changed. . .

Discipline was infrequent but fairly direct on the farm and, while I don't remember it ever being applied to our only sister, I love her anyway. We lived on a half-section with township roads running on the south and east ends of the property. At the juncture of these two roads grew some scraggly willow trees in the ditch. These willows made great bows for our bow and arrow escapades, but at discipline time, father would hand the offending one of us his jackknife and say "Go cut a switch."

The trick here was to not cut too small of one or father would go down himself and cut too big of one. It was pretty effective.

It went like this until the day I discovered I could outrun dad. We had this huge yard and after he had chased me for a while, he fell down on the lawn laughing. My father and I began to be friends after that day and I will always be grateful for his friendship as well as for his being my father.

Dad, of course, grew up during the great depression so he was very conservation conscious. This applied to water as much as it did money things. He mounted a rain barrel on the back roof of the chicken coop and once or twice a year he could have a shower as long as he remembered to wear his boots to and from the coop.

It doesn't seem fair to write about my childhood and not mention my mother. My mother wore combat boots. Really. She was a Marine during WW II and often talked about her experiences and her good friends. My sister later followed in mom's footsteps.

Everyone is supposed to rave about their mom's cooking. I always tell people about her beefsteak. The more you chewed it, the bigger it got. Her pheasant gravy was heavenly, however.

In fairness to mom, we never had electricity until I was two and running water when I was a little older. (And I helped install our phone line when I was a teenager.)

Mom was a brain and loved a good shaggy dog story. To this day, when I hear a great joke my first instinct is to call her but, of course, she's gone now.

I now have a new home town. About forty years ago, I moved to St. Paul, Minnesota. It is a strange little town in some ways. For example, in most towns, when you go from one block to another, you bump up the numbers a hundred. Not so in St. Paul. This gets really confusing in downtown when you are at Eleventh St. and the buildings are numbered in the three hundreds or so. Also, at one time at least, you could find North, South, East, and West Exchange Streets. I'm guessing this burg was founded by people who were afraid they would run out of numbers and names. (I don't know if this is related or not but the Flat Earth Society is still going strong here.)

Another thing about this town is snow. Snow absolutely mystifies the plow crews here. I imagine some drivers have put in entire careers without putting down the blade. It's as if all the snow plow drivers migrated from Hawaii. The good news is that the city is now ordering new plows with training blades. . .

St. Paul, as does all Minnesota, spends about nine months a year disproving the political myth of global warming. In fact, as a favor, here's a clue in case you're considering moving here: Any town that thinks it's a great idea to have a carnival in winter should be suspect. There is also a great misapplication of language in these parts. One day it can be thirty below and the next day twenty below. People here refer to that as warming up. Baloney. It's not warmer—it's just less cold.

One thing (among many) they did right was build the downtown by the beautiful river that flows through here. The suburb of Minneapolis didn't figure that one out.

I recently had to get a different car and I ended up at The Somali Pirates of Jackson Street. Like all the places we had been to that week, they had mastered the bait and switch as a team effort. It is a beautiful thing to watch as a team thing. At another place, the switch was thrown in by a waddling blonde in a skirt four sizes too tight on a rump four sizes too big. It would be easy to be mesmerized.

Getting back to St. Paul, there must be something in the regional water supply besides fluoride. There is a suburb directly south of St. Paul called West St. Paul. There is a suburb directly south of West St. Paul called South St. Paul instead of South West St. Paul.

On the other hand, on the East side of St. Paul is a park called Hillcrest Knoll. Aside from being doubly redundant, it is wrong. The park is in a cavity. It should at least have been named Hillcrest Knoll and Void.

Some of their naming attempts may, at first, seem oxymoronic yet, in the end, actually be prescient. On the near East Side is a short street called Sinnen. It terminates at the Sacred Heart Church.

I suppose the closest thing we could come to having bin sites in a large urban area in this timeframe would be food shelves. The great thing about these is they can be set up and run without government oversight. It's just citizens helping one another.

It would be nice to see these no longer needed, just as we no longer have local bin sites.

COMPOUND INTEREST

Several hundred years ago a group of religious moved to a large, mountainous island centered in a group of smaller ones.

This group lived for many years and prospered and grew in number. The only trouble was the occasional raid from tribes on neighboring islands.

Eventually there was a falling out over doctrinal interpretations of scripture and a cluster of the group decided to move away into their own compound. The leadership of this group thought it a good idea to build the compound as a fortress for security reasons. This they did and were impervious to the raids the original group was still experiencing.

Over time a second cluster emerged with still different doctrinal issues. They, too, decided to leave the original group and form their own colony. They also decided to build the fortress type of compound for security reasons. They, too, suffered no raids.

These two fortresses were the first known example of safe sects in history.

BARN

Probably the most striking building on our farm was the barn. It stood towards the back row of buildings, centered so as to give the impression of a monarch with visibility over the entire kingdom.

One of its key features was its wood shingle roof. Over the years, the roof acquired a mossy patina which became very slick after a rainfall. The west side of the barn featured two sections of roof, one at a steep forty-five degree angle and the lower portion at a much more reasonable gradient. On the west side of the barn was a hog pen.

After a rain, we would climb to the roof peak. This, in itself was an adventure. You had to go to the end of the roof and grip the overhang while you inched your way up. Once at the top, you carefully scooted toward the center of the barn until you were at the weathervane. Then, you faced westward, gathered your shoes under your rump and skied down the slope until you flew off the lower portion into the hog pen trying not to offend any residents there.

More often than not, you made the bulk of the trip on the seat of your jeans.

The barn had an awesome haymow. It was home to a remarkable collection of cats, barn swallows, mice and a big fat old rabbit named Rusty whom we placed up there. On sunny days, with the two big doors swung open, he would sit on the edge of the mow soaking up the sun.

It was in this haymow I killed my first animal.

With three sons and a farmer's income, it was tough for my parents to gift us in the manner we would have liked. Thus, we found ourselves tri-owners of a bicycle, a beebee gun, and, later on, a twenty gauge shotgun.

With the beebee gun, I shot a barn swallow one day. I picked it up and proudly carried it to my mom. Unexpectedly, she asked me why I did that. I didn't know what to answer. I thought that's what boys did.

At the time, television was replete with "Westerns." Many of the starring characters had unique weapons from Steve McQueen's "Mare's Laig" to Yancy Derringer's little pea shooter. There was gunplay on all three networks.

I have thought a lot about that little swallow over the years. Imagine being able to build a home in the midst of resources. And then, when it's time for the young ones to fly, so what if their first attempts are failures? There's lots of nice, soft hay for them to crash into.

But, mostly when I think about it, I rue the damage I did to an idyllic setting, a perfect family home. Are we innate killers or are we taught? Cain certainly had no mentor, at least of this world. Yet, we expect our soldiers to go off to war, kill other human beings and then return home as if nothing happened. I guess what we have that's innate is the ability to harden our souls and accept what's been done.

But, back to the barn.

The eastern portion of the barn was mostly for horses. We had a set of draft horses named Buck and Whitey, and a mare so old that she may have been the one Jesus rode into town on. Her name was Queenie. My cousin once stored his rodeo horse at our place. His (the horse's) name was Tobey. Once I thought it would be a good idea to get on Tobey's back while he was in the barn. This was not a good idea. The ceiling is not that far away from your head when he takes abucking.

After we no longer kept horses, this side of the barn served several purposes, one of them being a birthing site for sows. I remember watching one sow deliver her litter and, then, when I thought she was done, one more came out and was trapped in the afterbirth where it suffocated. I watched in horror but there was nothing I could have done. Baby pigs were, for me, a favorite animal—so full of energy.

One day, Dad brought home five five-gallon cans of red paint. The plan, I guess, was for us boys to repaint the barn. Here we were, two young teenage boys with no scaffolding, no safety harness, about five feet tall, with twenty five gallons of paint. How we were supposed to paint the upper reaches was never explained to us and the paint cans were never opened. They went the way of most things the day we had our auction.

The haymow served as our winter gymnasium. We put up a basketball hoop and, even though it was still very cold and the basketball would not bounce, we played hoops. The flooring of the haymow was a single layer of half-inch planks that liked to surprise us by breaking when we were least expecting it to. Carefully, you would pull your leg and foot back up through the hole.

The barn is gone now as are all the buildings and the sentinel windmill. The memories are still here and, truth to tell, most of them are good ones.

WEAVEBALL

With baseball going from the pastoral to the "Pasteural" and softball just plain going soft, it is time to recall that we started playing these games just for fun. What follows is an attempt to re-inject some of that back into a wonderful sport that is slowly but inexorably dying due to strikes, lockouts, slow pitch, and other crudities.

Fans, players, managers, owners, agents, and others, I give you WEAVEBALL. Weaveball is a scalable version of the old games that accommodates the idea that righties and lefties deserve equity on the ball fields.

To begin, all offensive motion is now counter-clockwise. Because the sequence never varies, we have first base, second base, and third base.

In Weaveball, left-handed hitters run clockwise and right-handed hitters still run counter-clockwise. We will rename the bases as left base, center base, and right base. As two runners are headed in opposite directions they can occupy the same bag. You could, in theory, have six runners on base. A Grand Salami now becomes a seven run homer.

But, the fun is only beginning. Imagine a bases-loaded situation such as this and a Joe Mauer coming to bat. No outfield wall is safe. And the ensuing chaos on the basepaths is a sight to behold. Broken bodies litter the infield as they have trouble dodging their teammates going in opposite directions. Frat keggers could be especially troublesome. Throw in three umpires who would finally be serving some purpose (clogging the base paths even more) and it should be (shudder) exciting. It will be NASCAR on the diamond. Even though Carl Edwards and Brad Keselowski might be on the same team, if they're going in opposite directions, get the stretchers ready.

Where Weaveball really shines, though, is in opportunities for managers to excel.

For example, you have a righty and a lefty both sitting on center base. If it is a close game and less than two outs, you might call a double steal. Even the best catcher in the business wouldn't be able to nail both of them.

Or, you have five base runners on and a chance for a big inning. Left base is open and Eddie Murray is coming up. Defensively, you bring in a pitcher to make Eddie bat left-handed so you can walk him to the open base. But, suppose Eddie is asked to bat right-handed and you have no place to put him. I can see an increase in value for switch-hitters who can hit both right-handed and left-handed pitching with success. And you may see a reemergence of ambidextrous pitchers.

The motto for Weaveball is "Just put it in play."

With a lot of runners on and a ball put into play the resulting ballet on the basepaths can only be named for a great old manager— the "Weave." Likewise, for those who forget where they are headed, we institute the term "Riegling." Think about it. Roy knows.

The tactical decisions necessary to play this game successfully are almost boundless. It is going to be especially tough for left-handed hitters to get reoriented. It will also be a challenge for defenders to remember which base to cover on bunts, which way(s) existing runners are going and even the umpires will have to be alert. The balk now replicates itself for left base.

Another element of this game is the opportunities for left-handed throwing players to also play all the infield positions, not just first base. This would also be true for catcher.

I would hate to see a designated wussy become part of this game.

Aluminum is forbidden.

In the United States, equipment shall be manufactured in the United States.

Also, a new sport needs a new anthem. This one shall be Fogerty's "Centerfield."

It's not that I don't like "Take me out to the Ballgame" but that song is about spectators. "Centerfield" is about actually playing the game and the joy of Weaveball will be in playing it.

Consider this. It would be possible to have nine people bat in an inning and no runs scored.

Imagine, Hoyt Wilhelm is pitching and there is a sextuple steal.

If the game doesn't sound complicated enough, let me propose the Rule of Sequence. This can best be described with an example.

Batters A, B, and C are left-handed hitters and each draws a walk. Batters D, E, and F are right-handed hitters and each also draw walks. The bases are now loaded. Batter G fulfills a lifelong dream of hitting the ball over the fence with six runners on. Under the Rule of Sequence, it makes a difference which runners cross home in which order. Technically, runners A, B, and C would cross, then D, E, and F before Sluggo can score.

Of course, the rule that would apply to home plate would also apply to center base and the corner bases. At the end of the game you could have some really stiff necks.

This example is too pristine for the real world as you would probably have some mix of right-handed and left-handed hitters in a normal sequence. This is where the real fun would begin and the real work for umpires would start.

I can see lots of opportunity here for confusion, chicanery, and argument. I can also see where it might bind up the game which I don't want to do. I offer it only as a corollary to the existing rule about passing runners in baseball and softball.

I'm not proposing to change America's grand old game. Although, after the designated hitter fiasco, ugly domes, lights at Wrigley, idiot commissioners with no craw whatsoever, and other "enhancements" such as the dreaded asterisk, not to mention "slow" pitch (softball's version of bowling) and extra outfielders in softball and NO bunting or stealing (okay, I did mention it.) I probably couldn't do much worse.

I'm just suggesting what sounds like a fun, picnic-type game on real grass and real dirt under the sun with good friends or friendly enemies.

I envision this tiny softball infield (fastpitch or modified fastpitch of course) with four infielders, six runners, two umpires and a battery all trying to get room to move or even breath. Ought to be a riot.

Still, at the professional baseball level. . .

FIGHTING MEDIOCRITY

Professional sport promotes and rewards mediocrity. For example—the draft. What an un-American approach to building a business.

However, I have two suggestions, for two different sports, that make minimal but meaningful differences to their product.

Years ago, there was a hockey team in town called the North Stars. They were going through a particularly bad stretch where nothing seemed to click. One night, they had to play the big, bad Boston Bruins. Somehow, the North Stars ended up on a power play. Boston had a young hotshot named Derek Sanderson who scored two short-handed goals on the same North Star power play. Would not this be an example of the essence of incompetence? Yet the Stars continued on their power play.

I think the rule should be changed to where a team is short-handed until the penalty time has expired or **a** goal is scored. Doesn't matter who scores it. If a team gives up a short-handed goal, they should be penalized for being terrible.

Similarly, in basketball, I would like to propose a change in statistical thinking. If a player misses the front end of a one and one, it goes in the books as oh for one. If you consider opportunity, however, it is oh for two and should be so recorded. For the money these people make, they should be given a realistic picture of their actual performance.

These changes could be implemented without changing the games at all.

WILLIE, THE MILKMAN

About forty years ago, after I had moved to St. Paul, I was in a bewailing mood one day at work. I was complaining about having to play slow-pitch softball with people (co-workers) who seemed non-chalant and even careless on the ball field. Combining this with my hating even the concept of slow-pitch and I was really building up a head of steam. I had grown up on fast pitch and had played on a series of good teams where the level of play was quite high.

As you can probably tell, this whole issue was MY problem.

A co-worker suggested I go out to his home town, about fifty miles away, and play on his team in a modified fast-pitch league. As the game was played, modified fast-pitch meant there was still bunting and stealing but the pitcher couldn't use a windmill or slingshot motion when pitching.

What you ended up with, then, were some really great "junk" pitchers.

The team I ended up on, called "The Squirrels," was comprised mostly of young guys who had grown up playing ball together. I was, at that time, the old guy. The team was competitive but still hadn't won "the big game" however that is described. That was about to change.

It was on this team that I was part of a triple play. As a runner. The batter, who shall remain nameless, still gets calls in the middle of the night about this.

One of the teams in our league had a pitcher named Willie. One year, he decided to switch teams and joined ours. Willie was a milkman by profession but what made him a legend was the fact he was two fingers short on his pitching hand. Sort of like Mordecai. Missing these fingers added some interesting aerodynamic twists to his pitches and it was nice to not have to face him any more.

Willie was a little on the heavy side but was extremely good natured. His favorite at-bat was drawing a walk.

Still another of the teams in our league—a good team, by the way, had an imposing first baseman named Hickey. Forty years ago we knew to put the shift on whenever he came up. I swear, it has since been recorded in the movie "Major League" when Heywood would come up. Hickey was our version of Ogie Oglethorpe. (As an aside, isn't it interesting that the part of Heywood was played by a pitcher?)

I don't remember Hickey really doing too much damage to us but put fear into our gloves.

Now, forty years later, I still wonder—"Did Hickey have a first name?"

RACK AND WRUIN

Thad was a professional poker player. He was one of a growing number of younger people with some technical training and education but a penchant for play. Poker provides for those who can play but who keep the ultimate goal in mind—payouts. Many play because they love to play, but they miss the goal repeatedly.

Like a number of his friends, he migrated to Las Vegas and, with some winnings, purchased a condo in the tower populated by many younger poker players. The tower itself might provide a great novel.

Lately, the poker tables had taken on a new look with the addition of young, lovely, and brainy female poker players who were, increasingly, a good match for the boys. One such poker terror was Kacey.

Poker players sometimes take on nicknames. Sometimes they don't choose them but come to them by some attribute they show at the table.

Kacey was Rack.

Thad could not beat Rack. He could not overcome the distraction of her attribute and, once, called her all in when he was holding a 2-4 off suit. Fortunately, since he was the one who called, he was allowed to muck his dogs and avoided some embarrassment.

Rack's good friend, Rita, had a different strain of nickname following her. She was on her third husband, all of them married at the time she came into their picture. Ultimately, her reputation as a home wrecker, led her to acquire the nickname Wruin.

Wruin played a different style of game. Patient, acquiescing, folding, biding her time. Men liked this style of play because it showed deference. It only dawned on them at the end that they were trapped.

She was a very hard read.

One time, Thad, as the big blind, was dealt a mixed marriage. Wruin was the small blind and was the only caller. The flop came a rainbow K-Q-J. Thad had hit the top two pair. The turn and river proved unexciting and Thad offered a pot sized bet.

Wruin, surprisingly, trebled his bet. Thad was confused. He finally concluded she was bluffing and went all-in. Wruin called and showed the bookends to Broadway—an ace-high straight.

"Nice flop." was all Thad could say as he hit the rail.

Phil was a gentle giant. He never used his imposing size at the table to intimidate anyone. His docility kept him from being a major force at the table but he valued his friendships more than anything. Sometimes he couldn't help winning because he got the cards but he rarely pushed. His acquired name became the I Fold Tower. The name was seldom used and never in direct communication however because, no one wanted to awaken a sleeping giant.

One of the old guys, Duffey, was a bit of a mystery to the poker group. He didn't blog or tweet, he never used a computer, he didn't own a cell phone. He wasn't exactly a Luddite but he felt technology peaked with wing windows.

Duffey loved poker. Any kind, and, over the many years, he had become very good at any kind. Duffey epitomized the problem younger players faced at the poker table when there is an older opponent. When you're young and confident, you don't want to be buried by an old fart in front of your peers. It becomes a delicate balance of respect and courage. Duffey took advantage of this whenever he could.

With a name like Duffey, you don't need a nickname.

Someone once made the mistake of asking Duffey how old he was and he made the mistake of answering:

"I'm a little gray around the edges, I guess."

"Edges are all you have left."

Thad enjoyed playing with Duffey because he loved the lore. Duffey had been around. And, Duffey seemed to take a shine to him. There are a few mentor relationships on the circuit and this bordered on that. Thad watched and paid and learned.

Duffey was old school in many ways. He dressed the part opting for a suit and tie instead of the ubiquitous poker bowling shirts so common on the tour. He chose not to sell his individuality.

Every morning he would stand in front of the mirror combing the memory of his hair while reciting the morning prayers he had said since childhood. His routine while in Las Vegas included always going to morning mass at the Our Lady of the Four-Corner Bingo just down the street from his favorite hotel.

Duffey's roots went back to his youth in the Black Hills. There, he grew up steeped in the legend of the Old Style Saloon Number Ten and it's most famous poker player, Wild Bill Hickok. It became a tradition for him to always play an ace—eight to the river if it wasn't too costly.

Tonight was a table stakes game that included some of his oldest friends in the game as well as several younger people. Chief among these was Paul. Paul held more bracelets than anyone but he had the least grace upon losing of any player in Vegas.

Once Paul was in a heads-up game against Amy King, part of the best brother-sister act in town. He began the match by offering the left-handed compliment "I wish I was playing your brother instead of you—he's less lucky." A couple hours later she had totally emasculated him and his stack all the while telling him what a great game he was playing, that she was just lucky, that he got a bad beat. He sucked it all up and, to this day, doesn't understand what a whupping he got that night.

Paul, in order to acquire some measure of adoration, tried to adopt the name "The Poker Pest." Most players referred to him as "Momma's

Boy." He was basically a one-trick pony but tonight there would be a variety of games at the table.

Mo Kemper was hosting the game. He was a property developer and was always looking for investors. His game didn't measure up to those showing up tonight but he was smart enough to recognize it. A lot of moneyed people think they can compete and learn harsh lessons if they're paying attention.

The game would be a one hundred thousand dollar buy-in with the winner taking half. The other half would go to the charity of the winner's choice.   In theory, at least, there should be some good press after it was over.

Mr. Kemper had invited Duffey, Thad, Rack and Wruin, Paul, Amy, Bill Carson who owned the Tucson Counts basketball team, and Duffey's best friend, Lloyd Branson. Mr. Carson was always a good sport about losing so they kept inviting him to the games.

The game would rotate. The first half hour was no-limit holdem. The second course would be five card draw. The next half-hour would be devoted to lowball followed by a split version of Omaha. There would then follow an hour break to snack and socialize. This was followed by the same routine in reverse order so the night would end with no-limit holdem. Kemper figured four hours should be enough to determine a winner.

The first few hands produced no surprises nor risk takers. In fact, for the first two hours everyone was sort of settling in and waiting for someone to take the alpha role. After the break, Bill and Wruin had slight chip leads.

About half-way through the second five card draw segment, it happened. Paul had been trying to insert himself into the lead role by informing everyone he owned the most bracelets and warning them he was also the best player in the other varieties. They let him keep talking.

On this particular hand, Bill was actually dealt quad nines with a three kicker. Paul was dealt a set of aces. Bill bet out and Paul called. As Bill took one card, Paul couldn't help but feel invincible, especially when he filled a boat on the draw. There was no way Bill could convert two pair or a flush or straight draw into something beating Paul's full house.

Again, Bill bet out and Paul offered a substantial raise. Bill thought for a moment and reraised. At this point Paul began to make remarks about donkeys and pigeons and amateurs and shoved all in, daring Bill to call. He did and, of course, Paul was beside himself at the result.

Paul was out. He couldn't believe it. No one at the table said anything. He didn't even say "thank you" to Mo as he made another graceless exit.

It took a few hands before the tension evaporated and the rest of the evening actually became enjoyable, if somewhat anticlimactic. Thad ended up winning the evening and the proceeds after sitting back and letting others dispose of Rack.

It takes a variety of strategies to win at poker and sometimes the best one is to not play.

LEBOWSKI

I recently watched "The Big Lebowski" and, while I enjoyed it somewhat, I have a feeling of lack of fulfillment about it. I finally realized why. At the end of the film this pointless cowboy (why was he even in the movie?) happens to mention there is a little Lebowski on the way.

Then it hit me. We need a sequel; "The Little Lebowski."

I imagine a four-year old baby, still in diapers, running around with a doobie in its mouth and holding a white Russian. Perhaps you could sign the kid who does the ETrade commercials.

He could go to day care where he acts like all little kids when adults are present but, say at naptime, he and all the other youngsters talk about NASCAR, broads, and football.

There could be another case of mistaken identity only it might involve a switched-at-birth theme. He could even be a real Lebowski offspring but from a different mother.

Get on it, will ya, Hollywood!

SEX ON THE DESK

D on't you just hate it when a writer uses a headline or title to entice you but the topic never shows up in the body of the work?

EDDIE

Sometime in the 1970s, my wife's younger brother, a St. Paul firefighter, was working a fire in an upscale part of town. Someone shot a picture of him coming down the ladder in full firefighter regalia, holding a child in his arms, giving mouth-to-mouth resuscitation as he came down the ladder. The picture caught fire, so to speak, and soon appeared on the cover of a national firefighter magazine and, shortly thereafter, Eddie was named "Firefighter of the Year."

Almost exactly a year later, in the same neighborhood, he was at another fire working the third floor of the premises when the flooring gave way and Eddie fell all the way to the basement. He landed at the feet of his captain who knew immediately something was wrong. There was. Eddie was to spend the rest of his days a quadriplegic.

This sudden turn of events had far-reaching effects on the whole family as well, most notably his beautiful wife who, probably, expected to spend many years raising children and grandchildren, not becoming a full-time caregiver to a two hundred pound invalid husband.

If you remember how the New York Firefighters stood together after the attacks in 2001, you have some idea how St. Paul's firefighters responded for Eddie and family. They built him a house! A magnificent property fully designed to make their lives as easy as possible.

Eddie and his wife had been thinking of buying a second home in Las Vegas. This dream was now gone. Many dreams were now gone as grim day-to-day reality set in. There were endless hours of therapy, learning how to move a mountain of a man for a sprite of a woman.

The firefighter brotherhood stood by him all his days, though, even posting an honor guard at his wake

When Eddie was still an active firefighter he was steering the tiller end of a long fire truck one day. As the truck went around the corner and Eddie prepared to steer the backend, the steering wheel came off and it and Eddie went sailing onto a parked car.

Eddie lived until almost eighty and died peacefully at home. His loyal wife these many years was at his bedside but, having early Alzheimer's, was at a loss to really understand.

The day of Eddie's funeral, as the cortege processed from the church to the cemetery, an inattentive driver blew through the signaled stop of the motorcycle escort and ran into the front driver side corner of the hearse.

We could only muse:

Never a dull moment with Eddie.

MY DREAM

Several years ago, I developed the annoying habit of assaulting my bride in the middle of night and in the middle of my dreams. She would have to wake me up, sometimes screaming for me to stop it. I would wake up to find I had been flailing away in my sleep in response to something I must have been dreaming about.

This, of course, bothered me. Probably bothered her, too.

After thinking about it, I decided to take control of my dreams. I learned to go to bed and think about the dream I chose, and, believe it or not, it has worked.

The dream takes place in a canyon off another canyon. I use the outer canyon as a buffer. I have buffalo ranging in the first or outer canyon.. Since I own the canyon, I consider this herd mine and eat heartily of bison meat.

The second canyon is reachable only by passing through the first. It contains a large combination farm and ranch. I raise cattle (feeder and dairy) and horses with separate barns. I also have some pigs and chickens. The pigs are housed in the lower level of the horse barn.

Some of the other outbuildings at the main ranch are a large machine shed, a two-story garage with a large mechanics work space inside, a main house, several other residences in which the ranch staff and their families dwell, and a centrally located library / schoolroom.

I had also recently purchased a lumber yard that was going out of business so I had to build a building to accommodate all of that inventory. Since this is a dream, my checks never bounce.

At the other end of the canyon is another large machine shed for farm implements to be stored at night as they're being used in the grain and corn fields away from the main farm.

The dream is built upon a conflicted premise. I hate winter. Yet, many episodes of the dream concern getting the ranch ready for winter. There is hay to put up (the small bales, not the big round ones). There is grain to harvest. The corn must be harvested and shelled. There are several silos on the ranch for storage. In addition, there are feed silos attached to the barns. All in all, it's a large operation.

Speaking of winter, a season I have serious issues with, I have decided to call a meeting of my ancestors when I get to where they are and make them explain to me why they would leave one frozen wasteland (Scandinavia) and emigrate to another (Eastern South Dakota). And they better not try to fog a religious freedom fastball by me. Unless it was the freedom to never go to church.

Anyway, getting back to the ranch, the construction of all the buildings is unique. They all have a layer of lead sheeting on their shells. Even all the windows have a lead component. At this stage of my life, based upon what I've observed about our government, I am going for privacy here. I don't want drones swooping down in the middle of the night spying on us.

The ranch contains quite a number of secrets, many of them underground.

The library / schoolroom, which is attached to the main house, is also a "weather room." There are many windows facing the North and West and we all enjoy gathering there to watch the storms roll in. During especially long, overnight storms, the kids of the ranch all bring their sleeping bags over and stay the night watching the weather.

The ranch is very remote and very private and, consequently, there is a high degree of self sufficiency to it. Almost all of our goods are grown or raised there. We have our own wells and a well-managed septic system. All the main roads are forty ton-rated as we have tractor trailers hauling grain, livestock, feed, and other commodities.

Speaking of commodities, we have two working oil wells on the property with tanks and a steady stream of truck traffic carting the stuff away. There is also natural gas underground but we haven't decided how to transmit it yet.

I have really good, trustworthy people working with me on this operation. There are experienced ranch hands and farmers, carpenters and mechanics to name a few. I have no illegals working for me.

I call the outer canyon "Big Parc" and the inner one "Little Parc." I have had both of them infested with a network of Piezo cables, calibrated to a mapping system, so I can detect intruders. Beneath the library is a large control room with many computer and video screens. The property has a lot of miniature cameras planted about as well. Right now, this system pays for itself almost nightly as I capture on video, bear and wolves and other predators poking around the farm. It is a practice on this site to always make sure all livestock, machinery, vehicles, tools, pets, toys, whatever, are stowed away each evening.

I have lately been thinking about building a crypt for deceased family members. It would be a huge undertaking (no pun intended) and requires a pretty elaborate design. It would be a little way up the mountainside from the main house in a tree blessed setting. The great thing for this project is it has let me think about all my known ancestors. Also many of the living whose permissions I would need to move the deceased family members here.

Inside the horse barn is a tackroom. At the back of this room is a secret button which, when pushed, allows a part of the back wall to swing out and reveal a room full of ordnance. Rifles, pistols, probably some things I'm not supposed to have. Kids growing up on the ranch will have to take firearms training. They will all be comfortable sitting atop a horse.

Inside the ordnance cubbyhole is another secret button that opens a panel that leads to a stairway which is actually within a silo at the back of the barn. The stairway leads to an underground tunnel system that connects all buildings.

I have decided to build a large structure in Big Parc to store a supply of alfalfa for the Bison to eat when the winter snow gets especially deep. The building would also house a plow that I will use to create space to distribute the hay.

I will have a water supply for the bison that is heated just enough to keep the tanked water thawed.

I am constantly stocking up on supplies. Don't know where this springs from, perhaps all the remembrances of the depression I grew up listening to.

One of my favorite aunts, upon passing away, had been found hoarding toilet paper in her house. There were rolls everywhere. Turns out she had had the habit of listening to Johnny Carson and, one night, his monologue included a reference to an upcoming toilet paper shortage. It was intended as a joke but my aunt and, I'm sure, many other elders took it to heart.

In the same way, I buy up lots of blankets and bedding. My memory of childhood in the wintertime was frost-covered windows and we would grab our duds in the morning and run downstairs to get dressed by the little stove. Even today, I feel naked with only one blanket. I like lots of them, especially heavy ones. Don't try to pacify me with a plug-in variety.

The whole idea here, I suppose, is to try and recreate my earlier life by having a place big enough to support my entire known family, with the crypt, to house all the deceased ones, and give the young ones good memories and a safe environment to grow up in.

Do you have a dream?

Jewels

Cliff and Rita had been married for thirty seven years so Rita was pretty sure something was going on with Cliff. Theirs was a happy marriage that had produced a son, Sam, who doted on his parents. Lately, Cliff had seemed listless and seemed to be going to the bathroom more often than he used to.

Gingerly, because she knew he hated doctors, she broached the subject of him having a check up. It helped her argument that he was going to be sixty soon so she dressed up the idea as a present to himself to have one last physical. An appointment with Dr. Burns was agreed to.

At the conclusion of his physical they were in a conference room with the doctor.

"Cliff, it looks pretty good pending some lab results. I am a little concerned that you have an enlarged prostate that may be precancerous. I'd like you to consider having it removed as a precaution."

"No way, Doc. All the parts of my body that aren't already cancerous are precancerous, too, like my brain and my limbs and my liver—why don't we remove them also?"

"No need to be upset, Cliff."

"Tell me something, Doc—To the best of your knowledge, has a surgeon ever cured anybody?"

"Clifford!" interjected Rita. "The doctor is only doing his job. Don't be so rude."

Cliff adroitly ignored her. "Thanks for your time, Doc."

On their way to the pickup, Cliff could tell Rita was upset with him.

"What's wrong?" asked Cliff as they motored back to the farm.

"Nothing. I just want you to live. That's all." She replied although the sarcasm failed to get traction.

"Hey—he said I'm okay."

"You need to have your prostate removed." She pressed.

"Do you know what that would mean for us?" he asked, almost angrily.

"Of course I know. And I have really loved our life. I want to continue having a life with you."

"For me it would be a lot less of a life."

They kept it up until they got home and went their separate ways doing chores.

Two days later, Doctor Burns called Cliff. "I've got some news from the lab reports. You seem to have a tumor on one of your kidneys. We should get together and make a plan."

The plan they agreed to was to remove the kidney with the tumor since he would still have one good kidney left. He was instructed that he might want to consider scaling back his farming workload while he recovered and, perhaps, permanently.

Two days after the surgery, when the anesthetic fog had mostly lifted, Doc Burns stopped by.

"I have good news, Cliff, the cancer was totally isolated to the one kidney so you are now cancer free."

"That's wonderful, Doc, when can I go home?"

"Not for a few days, Cliff. There's something else. I removed your prostate at the same time. It was enlarged."

"You what? You fucking butchers are all alike. Get out of here!"

"Cliff, it was the most expedient thing to do. If you had to go back for a second surgery later it would have been much more costly."

"I'm going to sue you for performing unpermitted surgery! I'll have your license."

"But Cliff, it was permitted. Rita okayed it after I explained the details."

"Rita? She had no right. I'll sue you and divorce her, then kill you both!"

"Cliff, you're not going to kill anybody.

"Get out of here, you bastard!"

Cliff reached for the light button and, when the attendant arrived, announced he wanted "out of here." The aide said he would need the Doctor's permission which set him off again. Cliff threatened to pull out all his drains and tubes if they wouldn't help him.

It was at this point that Rita arrived trying to show sunshine and happiness, unaware he knew of her deed. He really let her have it and she ran from the ward crying. He didn't care in the least.

After the aide removed the tubes and drains and bandaged him up, Cliff called Sam for a ride home. As he was slowly getting dressed the doctor returned to try to encourage him to remain in the hospital for a few more days just to be safe. Cliff went on dressing ignoring the doctor's very presence. He thanked the aide and left the ward heading toward the lobby.

After Sam dropped him off at their small farm, Cliff went to the garage and got into his pickup and left. He made several stops and purchases before sundown.

Rita hadn't heard from Cliff for a couple of days. She was still somewhat mad at Sam for going to get him at the hospital but couldn't expect him to have to choose sides.

She decided to walk out to the road and get the mail. In the mailbox, among other mail, was a small package. There was no return address so she returned to the house somewhat mystified. Setting aside the other mail, she opened the little package. Whatever it was, it was packed in soft cotton.

As she peeled away the cotton and saw what it was, she gave out a shriek. Inside was a scrotum complete with testicles. She fell to the floor in a faint.

After her funeral service, Sam was walking around the homestead trying to recapture good memories from the place. He spied the oak tree they had planted together on their wedding day. They had told him the story many times. It had flourished under their care as had he.

As he walked up to it one last time he failed to notice a small patch of freshly upturned soil.

TESTAMENT

Shortly after my bride and I were first married, I was having difficulty sleeping one night due to the shakes and shivers. I didn't want to wake her so I went out to the couch to try and sleep. First, I said a little prayer thanking God for my discomfort and asking that it be used to glorify His name and could it possibly take the place of someone else's discomfort or pain.

That was all I asked.

Immediately, it seemed, I was calm, quieted, warm. I laid there waiting for the symptoms to return but they never did.

Reflection has made me aware of other "interventions" on my behalf.

When my son was about a month old, I was getting a little tired of the fact he seemed to cry a lot. He had no temperature or anything so we just thought he was crabby baby. One day, I was left at home alone with him when he started in again. Nothing I did could soothe him. Finally, I decided to take a shower with him hoping it would get his mind off his crying.

It was in the shower I noticed a bulge in his lower right abdomen. Hernia.

It is only recently I realized what (or Who) gave me the notion to go into the shower with him.

Sometimes, God has answered a prayer I wasn't smart enough to pray.

When my bride and I were courting, it was my style to drive with my left hand on the wheel and my right arm around her shoulder. One night we were on a freeway doing about seventy when my right arm felt very tired. I decided to change its position so I put the right hand on the wheel along with the left.

About two minutes later we had a blowout.

Elsewhere in this tome I have related the story of my brother.

If I were to title this next event, perhaps it would be "My Bonnie Lies."

I was recently betrayed by a person I had considered a very good friend, one I had placed great trust and confidence in. As I struggled with the anger and hurt and sadness, one day, a little voice said to me "Forgive her."

I have learned to pay attention to this voice over the years and so I did as it told me—I forgave her.

I think we tend to think the only beneficiary of forgiveness is the forgiven one. In this case I will probably never know. But almost immediately after forgiving her, my anger disappeared and, in fact, I have been sleeping peacefully and restfully ever since.

Listen to the voice.

When I begin to try to catalogue all the incidents in my life that have had such signal moments, it gets a little overwhelming. I begin to get the feeling we're here for a purpose and we're being looked out for until we've accomplished it.

There are events in my life past that, even today, I can't begin to write about because they are still hard to accept. I just have to allow that God is in charge and knows what's best.

I think it would be a good thing for everyone to spend some time reflecting on their past and note these kinds of moments. There are those whose experience must seem all bad but, I believe there's something at work for them going on here.

I would also encourage people to share their experiences. That's, essentially what this book is all about. Don't be afraid to talk about it. And, don't worry about being "politically correct."

TEST PATTERN

Dexter was dead and, the curious thing was, he knew it. Here he was sitting upright in his living room chair in front of the fairly new Philco television set he had purchased so he could keep up with the neighbors.

He wasn't what you'd call a social animal, he mostly stayed by himself. And, he only went to work because it was expected, even though his frugality had made him comfortable.

As he stared straight ahead he was aware he could see the television and could identify the people in the tube. Jack Paar's lips were moving, people were laughing, but the voices seemed so far away.

"This is odd," he thought. He then started to scan the rest of the room and realized his eyeballs were immobile but he could see around the entire room. Everything seemed to be in place. He decided to get up but couldn't move his body. Yet, he was able to relocate somehow, to where he wanted to go. He was able to move around his entire apartment this way but could not feel anything.

"I might as well just go back to my easy chair", he thought "until someone comes and finds me. Besides, my body is still there."

In time, Jack Paar went off the air. In fact, everything went off the air and this test pattern appeared on the screen for the duration of the night.

It was then that Dexter realized we all end up in test pattern mode after it's over. We've had our say, told our jokes, made our children, said our prayers. Whether or not these things were done satisfactorily doesn't matter after the test pattern comes on. You can't go back and change anything. There is no mulligan.

You have to wait for the reviews.

YOUR NIGHTMARE

C an you feel the pull? Are you starting to get dizzy? It's called the Coriolis Effect. Originally, this referred to the curving deflection of winds caused by the Earth's rotation[1] but its meaning has broadened to also mean the cyclonic effect of a toilet flushing. What you are feeling, what you are experiencing is the flushing of moral values down the drain. The pull is world-wide and, I fear, unstoppable.

Let me tell you about your nightmare. It starts when I am elected President. Not that this will ever happen (Heck, I don't even vote anymore!)—but for this discussion you must assume it can.

In 2008 we had a president with an embarrassing approval rating. His second term was ending so we were asked to select his replacement from a group with an even lower rating. What kind of choice was that? Tell the truth now—had you ever heard of the Democratic candidate before 2006? Me neither, although, to be fair, we should probably count him as "present." And his opponent sits on the fence of issues so tightly he has slivers in his crack.

Article I, Section 8 of the Constitution says that the Congress shall have the authority to make all Laws which shall be necessary and proper for carrying into Execution the foregoing Powers, and all other Powers vested by this Constitution in the Government of the United States, or in any Department or Officer thereof.

Article III creates the Supreme Court but does not empower it to make laws. Yet, for the last fifty years or so, Congress has abdicated their role in favor of being nothing more than pork farmers. (No disrespect intended to genuine pork farmers here.)

1. The New York Public Library Science Desk Reference (1995); Pg. 452

The nightmare, then, is this: I will begin, on a case by case basis, the review of all Supreme Court rulings that became this country's de facto laws with the intent of setting aside all such decisions as not being within the purview of the court itself. Further, I will not accept their (the court's) argument to decide the merits of my actions because of their conflict of interest. I intend to take this at least as far back as my four years will allow. (I do not intend to run for reelection.)

At this point I should tell you I once voted for both Clinton and his successor. I realize, in hindsight, that this makes me not only an idiot but a political slut. Please forgive me—it won't happen again.

The intent is to put Congress on the spot and make them responsible for what they were elected for. Just to make it interesting, I would revisit the issue of states rights with an inherent bent to allow them (and, no, I don't believe in slavery).

This whole discussion freely concedes I am no attorney and, even more freely, asserts I am grateful for that. But you don't have to be an attorney to see the moral sewer that has become our little planet. In fact, I would think being an attorney would cause blinders to appear when they observe this world. They would look at things in the context of whether or not things are legal without regard to the moral effect. I don't have any idea what Congress's excuse would be.

A large part of the fetid odor that exists is our communication vehicles. We have assorted media all competing for your approval and, I think, even using their polling data to help them decide what is newsworthy. And they are sheep. As I've said, I no longer vote but I found it telling how all the media seemed to think Governor Palin was unqualified because she was only a governor. I don't recall such heartfelt concerns when the ACLU sphincter kissing tank commander from Massachusetts, the thong snapper from Arkansas, the peanut pansy from

Georgia, the idiot Pinocchio from Texas, the goofy actor from California, the "Nolo Contendre zero from Maryland all ran. So what is the common denominator here? They're all men. And who runs the media? Men and women who wish they were men. And, of course, men seldom question the capabilities of other men. It's kind of like the map thing—men never get lost. . .

Did I mention we're pulling out of the U. N.? And, even though they have a free building to use on prime U. S. property, I will be encouraging them to move to somewhere else. Or else, start paying taxes for services rendered. I can't imagine a bigger eunuch than the U. N..

I am issuing an executive order stating that the U. S. Census shall be done on a post card and the only questions allowed is "How many individuals live in this house?". That's it. None of this sociological, advertising-based, snooping that is now allowed. None of the rest of this crap is any of the government's business.

We are not going to be part of the new world order. We are going to be the United States of America. A sovereign nation.

The first budget I sign will be for no more than eighty percent of the previous year's budget. Each year will follow the same script. By the end of my fourth year, we will be spending no more than forty one percent of what we spent when I started. The word "trillion" will disappear from our budgetary lexicon. We can do this. Any spending bill that lands on my desk with items included that do not relate to the purpose of the bill will be vetoed outright. I will veto the entire bill for just one transgression. No more bridges to nowhere.

This is a simplified, two-fold effort to both reduce spending and reduce this monstrous thing we call a government. Eventually, entire bureaus, maybe even departments would be axed.

At the same time I am interested in building up our nation. I would like to see Puerto Rico finally become a state. I would also begin discussions with Mexico about folding them into the United States with their thirty one states. The idea here is to eliminate the border issue and move it southward where it will be a lot smaller problem. This will also give the U. S. the opportunity to wreak havoc on the Mexican drug industry. We will also gain valuable shore line on the East and West for naval purposes. Finally, on the statehood front, I would like to make overtures to Denmark concerning the possible acquisition of Greenland. Again, there would be military advantages to this, I believe.

Are we still worried about Cuba? With Puerto Rico, Yucatan, and Florida as jumping off points to deal with them, I don't believe they will be a problem. (And, with both Alaska and Greenland in the mix, we have Canada practically surrounded!) (If you think this is crazy, where do you think the oil sands are? The yellowcake? The water?)

Of course, I would have to start my own party. There's little to choose from given the present characters. Sometimes people associate the word "liberal" with the democrats. There are no liberals in the democratic party. A liberal would be a person open to new ideas, to considering all points of view. Democrats march in lockstep to whatever marching orders are given them. No tugging on the reins here.

Sometimes people associate the word "conservative" with republicans. I wonder why that is. The last republican president we had acted as if he had never heard of the word.

Republicans are anti-worker (see Reagan). Democrats love the worker until they get their votes. Then, they take the worker vote to mean we all want more and bigger government.

And the two parties work together marvelously. I give you this example. Reagan, conveniently forgetting that he once led a labor union, fired all the air traffic controllers. His successor, supposedly representing the party of the worker, then named an airport after this idiot. Did the media catch this irony?

My party will be called "conservertebrates." Conservatives with backbone. These will be our guiding principles:

Small Government		Strong Defense
Pro Worker		Pro Business
Pro Life	Pro Growth	Low Taxes
Drilling	Pro Soldier	Self-sufficiency

I don't care if Hollywood nor Broadway support me—I won't go to their parties and love fests. Lobbyists and other looters will be shot on sight.

We will not rescue companies or industries. You mess your bed—you sleep in it. There is such a disconnect between Wall Street and the real world anyway that I fear we have devolved the world's first perpendicular universe.

There will be no wholesale spying on our own citizens. There will be the right to bear arms unless you are a felon or Dick Cheney (same thing).

I will work for a constitutional amendment to limit terms of congress people (four two-year terms), senators (two six-year terms), and the Supreme Court (ten years).

Pass the sleeping pills.

RICOCHET ROOM

"Has the jury reached a verdict?" Judge Thomas Daly asked the foreman. He was internally angry because, even if they found the defendant guilty, he was limited in his ability to mete out appropriate punishment. Over time he had grown sick of murderers getting off with sentences tied to lesser charges.

"We have, your honor. We, the jury, find the defendant Charles Reno Alverez guilty of second degree murder."

Second degree murder. What a sham. Alverez deliberately and with malice aforethought marked and murdered his victim with cold blooded precision. True, the victim was a member of a rival gang but it was premeditated murder just the same thought the judge.

Connor County where the good judge presided was faced with a growing gang-related nightmare. He, himself was starting to feel the heat politically. What was needed was a message and soon.

The judge walked into Kemper's Bar later that week on a mission of construction. He was looking for Per Jorgenson, probably the last remaining blacksmith in Connor County. He knew his friend, Per, liked to stop by Kemper's on his way home Friday nights.

Eventually, the huge Swede showed up with haloos all around the bar. He saw his friend, Tom, sitting at a table in the corner and went over to say "Hi". The judge offered a seat and Per took it, sensing that Tom wanted to talk about something.

After the wait person had taken their order, Tom handed Per a set of drawings to look at. Per studied them for a few moments and then asked "Do you want me to build this?" This was a room made out of three fourth inch thick steel with thirty two sides, almost soccer ball shaped.

On the inside of the room were pyramids welded to many of the panels. The tips were shown to be rounded off.

On the bottom panel was a drain.

The room had several small windows that worked by opening a cover panel. Two of the windows had an electrical source. Two of the panels, on opposite sides, could be swung open.

"What the hell is this anyway?" asked Per.

"It's a device for justice." answered Tom.

"How does it work, then?" asked Per, squinting at the drawing again in the dim light.

"I'd rather not say at this time, Per." said Tom. "Can you build it? I have a warehouse we can construct it in down by the water."

Per was still looking at the plan. "What's this drain for?"

"Cleaning up."

Tom cleared his throat. "Can you get me a quote for time and materials by the end of next week?"

"Sure. There will be a lot of preliminary work what with cutting all the pieces to size."

"One more thing, Per. It's kind of a confidential project."

"I see."

"I'll get back to you next week with a quote, Tom."

The following Thursday evening, Tom called Per to confirm the meeting and to suggest they meet in Tom's house.

When Per arrived, he was surprised to also find Ben Stevenson there. Ben was a master carpenter who had lost a son to violence two years prior.

Tom began to lay out his vision for the project. About halfway through the presentation Tom had to finally let on the reason for the project.

It was at this juncture that Tom offered them both the opportunity to withdraw. He was pretty sure Ben wouldn't and Per, who was as apolitical as they come, thought for only a couple of moments before deciding to continue.

Per said he could start cutting the pieces the coming week and would have them ready by Wednesday. Ben, meanwhile, would acquire the other materials needed and it was agreed to meet at the dockside warehouse on Friday afternoon and unload the supplies. At this point they were still only a cabal of three. Tom brought the few plumbing supplies they figured the item would need.

The following week, Per and Ben practically moved into the warehouse. Because the metal slabs were so heavy, it worked much better to have two people hoisting them. Per would do two quick spot welds on each contact point to hold the piece in place. Then, while he would weld the entirety of all the borders by himself, Ben would work on construction of the outside façade which included copious soundproofing.

It took three and a half weeks but when it was finished it was as rugged as Tom had hoped. Tom paid off Per and Ben and thanked them for their services.

With the one conspiracy completed, it was time to create another. This involved co-opting the services of a seasoned deputy and two auxiliary policemen who believed their service in this endeavor would get them promoted to full-time employment as deputies. Tom and Dale, the deputy, did nothing to discourage this assumption.

It was time to test the room.

A mannequin was installed, standing on the bottom panel. The first test was using dum-dums, a kind of bullet that flattened out whenever it ran into an obstruction tougher than it was. These slugs cause great bodily harm if they have a chance to spread out first. The walls of the ricochet room were ideal for this.

The first slug expended its whole bundle of energy without once hitting the mannequin. Not the result they were expecting. Another facet of the testing showed the soundproofing was more than adequate.

A second dum-dum was fired into the room at a different angle. This one caught the mannequin in the leg after several redirects.

The group considered what was happening and whether or not they should proceed to steel jacketed slugs. Dale offered the opinion that the more slugs it took to finish off the perp, the better because it would give him time to think. This was an idea Tom hadn't really considered. However, the more he thought about it, the better he liked it.

The test with the tougher steel jacketed slugs yielded similar results. They even tried a couple of experiments using simultaneous shots.

Tom was ready and eager to put the tool to the test in a practical way. He had plenty of fodder to stock the room with.

His first was a drug kingpin that was responsible for the death of at least seven people, five of them innocent bystanders. He was incarcerated at the moment for an assault charge while detectives pursued leads to link to him the more serious charges. The judge didn't want to have to try this guy more than once.

The deputy and the auxiliary officers removed him from his cell on the basis of a spurious document from Tom. The killer, Shanks by name, was under the impression he was just going to another pretrial hearing.

In a way, he was.

Handcuffed and shackled, he sat quietly in the back of the cruiser. One of the auxiliary officers placed a hood over the head of Shanks as soon as they were a couple of blocks from the jail. When they ended up dockside, he grew restless and agitated and began to scream at them. They simply ignored him and pulled into the bay of the warehouse where the judge was waiting.

The four of them managed to get Shanks into the somewhat crowded steel echo chamber. They forced him to sit on a chair which they chained him to. They then all left but the Deputy who pulled off the hood. He then left and the door closed with an ominous clang.

Shanks looked around the room. There was one light on and all he could see were angled walls with a bunch of cones on them. All of a sudden, a voice came over some hidden speaker: "Shanks, you are here to die. You had fun killing _____, now we're going to have fun killing you. These walls are plate steel. We will be firing bullets into the room one at a time. If, by the time the bullet has spent it's energy you're still breathing, we will fire another—at a different angle. You are the grand prize winner and the prize you have won is to be the first to use the Ricochet Room."

The light went out.

After a short pause, Shanks could hear a squeak as if a rusty-hinged door was opening. In fact, one was.

"Bang!"

The noise was deafening.

This bullet made its circuits without harm to Shanks. He began to feel a little invincible.

The light came on, then , quickly off.

"Bang!"

This time, the dum-dum found its mark striking Shanks in the left temple and killing him instantly.

The light came on.

The body and the weapon were placed in a bag and put into the trunk of the cruiser. The judge, meanwhile, was hosing down the apparatus. He picked up the stray bullet and put it in his pocket.

Later that evening, the deputy and his helpers, carried Shanks back to his cell and left the gun beside him replacing one of the bullets. It had been the gun Shanks used in committing his own murder and his prints were already on it. How he managed to get the same gun back so he could commit suicide was never explained.

In reviewing the evening, the Judge felt like something was missing. Sure, justice was served. Sure, they saved untold thousands of taxpayers' dollars. Sure, the perp would never kill again.

At last, it hit him. When done this way, there is no lesson to share. No warning to send. His training in the judicial sciences was telling him this was needed. The iron-fisted judge in him won out, however, and he realized, in his mind at least, it's not the court's job to give lessons. It should focus on justice and, secondly, public safety.

To hell with lessons.

ENDS AND ODDS

Today I am not proud of what I did yesterday when I was proud.

***

It has always bothered me that the word "palindrome" isn't one.

***

I'm sort of troubled by the fact that the word "Verb" is a noun.

***

Of all the people old enough to remember Nixon's ordeal, I seem to be the only one who finds it interesting that, during Clinton's impeachment, no one wanted to see the smoking gun.

***

The great thing about faith is that it relieves you of the burden of intellect.

***

If "the moment is right," why are they in separate tubs?

***

There is no Artificial Intelligence, only dummy data.

***

People complain that the world is going to heck in a hand basket. Let's get real here. We started out with paradise and change is constant. If paradise changes, then, and, if paradise is the ideal, change can only make it worse.

***

I no longer think zoos are a good idea.

***

This just in: Archeologists in Tanzania have unearthed the world's very first glacier. Turns out, it was a government. . .

***

If you were to look at me or my picture you might conclude I'm as old as the calendar says I am. I prefer, however, to tell people that I'm really twenty nine—it's just that the winters have been hard on me.

***

We have eliminated slavery but have "human resources." Money is a resource. Tools are a resource. Workers are people. It gets worse. Some unenlightened companies use the term "Human Capital." How unfeeling is that?

***

"He has numbered the hairs upon my head." But where did they go? Will those who get to heaven find a lawn of curly and straight red or black or brown or blond hair instead of grass?

***

I know I'm old because now, when my wife hollers at me "Stick it in your ear!" she's talking about my hearing aid.

***

I will never understand the phrase: "I'll have a large Diet Soda."

***

Remember the "Cold War?" Tell me—Do you still think we won?

***

His weekly paycheck tells him what he already knows
That money comes and money goes but, mostly, it just goes.
Our economic future is once again foretold
Put your money in a coffee can—the banks are going to fold.

***

Nobody loves free-range chickens as much as the fox.

***

Call the doctor? Call the doctor? Are you kidding? If I have an erection that lasts more than four and a half hours, I'm not calling the doctor. I'm calling more women!

***

I had this dream I was going to a comedy club to see two comedians—Steven Wright and Rita Rudner. You can just imagine the excitement.

***

Since time began, it has not been a good idea to use the words "Baseball" and "Integrity" in the same sentence. It is now 2010 and nothing has changed. . .

***

Maybe Old Yeller didn't have rabies. Maybe he was just another pit bull.

***

NUANCES

YEAR

It's State Fair time.

It snuck up again.

It seems like every year it comes 'round quicker.

I once read where Einstein is to blame for this.

Something about time speeding up as we get older.

Probably the first law of temporal dynamics.

CAVE

We are packing the cave with supplies.
War is coming.
War is coming to us.
We will not have go "off" to fight it.

We have lost our jobs.
We have lost our homes.
We have lost our income.
We have lost our daily lives.

The poverty rate is climbing.
Yet, the political pigs at the public trough
Ignore our pleas.
They try to stifle us with "stimulus."

The banks are too big to fail.
I am only one vote.
I am too small to succeed.
I have no PAC money.

We are packing the cave with supplies.
Food, bedding, toiletries
Guns, ammo, rockets
War is coming to us.

LEARNING CURVES

I want to spend the rest of my life
Exploring your topography.
I will memorize your contour lines
And blend with your landscape.

We are complementary maps
With similar desires.
We have different points of origin
Yet, the same sweet goal.

You would make cartography an art
By virtue of your beauty
A subject like none other
A map of wonderland

LONE WOLF

I was Akela, who ran with the pack
I was their leader who never looked back
I could outrun them all as I led the way
To that evening's supper, followed by play.

We howled at the moon and the moon smiled right back
I took on all comers who wanted my pack
I won many battles for my females so fine
But now, I'm a lone wolf—they're no longer mine.

My teeth are wore down, my legs go real slow
I will have trouble this winter in the heavy wet snow
I will probably get hungry and then slowly die
But, I've had a great run so there's no need to cry.

My sons and my daughters are doing quite well
In packs of their own now my story they tell
I was Akela, who ran with the pack
I was their leader who never looked back

FROSTBITE

Steam is rising from the lake—the geese are asking "Why?"
Hockey boards are going up—there's winter in the sky.
The trees have given it their all but now are standing bare.
The grass is brown, the acorns stashed, the clues are everywhere.

The wind is telling us "Beware—the time is drawing near
When the unprepared will lose the things they've always held so dear.
So, make your peace and say your prayers and give to God your
worldly cares
And be precise when ordering your personal affairs

Winter is a metaphor for pulling in your horns
For giving thanks for all your nights and also for your morns
We come in alone to this cruel world and outward so we go
To the promised land we all can have that's free of cold and snow.

DEER HUNTER

THEME

Mikey, Steve, and Nick go off to
fight the bloody Cong
Attrition being what it is, the
threesome wasn't long
Shattered limbs, a crazied brain,
contribute to the math
Their journey splits them up—
it seems more ways than one
Their oneness camaraderie now gone
The threesome is reduced by half.

STORY

Shine your boots and oil your gun
Tonight the deer hunter is having fun
Losing himself in the hills and woods
Tracking, listening, moving, still
Battle of nerves, test of will
Sight him in—you've got the goods.

Go off to war. It's just the same.
With antlerless two-legged game
The rules have changed a little bit
But, you adapt, you're good at that
The trick is knowing where they're at
Before they hit.

The trigger game will haunt your life
Each "Click" will hit you as a knife
Each "Bang" as if it were your head
At home, the quarry didn't shoot back
At home, the trophy was a rack
At home, you wouldn't end up dead.

Silent Day

Today, I do not wish to speak
Nor sing your song
Nor say my prayers.

It is quiet that I long for
My own as well as yours
A nod, perhaps

I will say my prayers within my heart
And know your song tomorrow.
This quiet is an experiment.

The world is noisome
Never listening
Always vying to be first.

Let me hear my God today.
Let me see my neighbors' need.
Let me know the path to take.

Tomorrow I will return
To the cacophony.
I will grit my teeth.

ZIG ZAG

We gambol 'round the room
Me chasing the dream
You giggling as you run
My plan has always been
To chase you 'til you catch me.

We may need a bigger room
I'm getting the hang of this
I use the corners to my advantage
I think you know this
And run there on purpose.

At the time I found you
I was about ready to give up.
Then, like a miracle, I found you
Hiding behind some friends.
I drew you out with chocolate.

At first we became friends
But, I knew all along
It was more than that.
Now we gambol, now we love
And I still buy chocolate.

HIGH RISK

As we dance the minuet of courtship
Atop the foaming rushing rapids
We avoid the fearsome "L" word
As if it was the looming falls ahead.

Sweet Dee. Sweet Dee. Come dance with me
Upon the solid shore of love
I'll bring you daisies for your hair
And whisper all my secret thoughts of you

We listen to the music of our hearts
And contemplate each other's loving web
I ache to rush to yours and, there,
Be free from all the traps and trappings of my life.

UNREQUITED

Here I am and there you are
How can I bridge a span so far?
How can I make you love me, dear
When here I am and there you are?

There you are and here I be.
Caring, waiting patiently
With troubled mind and aching heart
And there you are and here I be.

If I was here and you were here
I know I'd lack the heart held dear
You have another on your mind
Though I was here and you were here.

So, there you are and here I am
And, though I really give a damn
I cannot change what's in your heart
So, there you are and here I am.

STRUCTURE

Today is the day you die.
You are a soldier
U. S. Corporal
Today you will be point.
A Sergeant will pick you.

He reports to a Lieutenant
With a degree in Sociology.
His Captain is from a college
Where he studied ROTC.
He earned some money that way.

The Major is on her second tour
And is tougher this time around.
Her Colonel has wounds from two other wars
He can't remember who won.
It was probably a tie.

The General has a wide assignment
Fighting the war and making friends
His bigger General oversees both current wars.
Congress wants to know how much
And the President feels the heat.

Today is the day you die.
All those in the chain above you
Have made you the leader
You of the lowest rank
Have been chosen as the Judas goat

Your parents will never understand
(Especially when we quit the war)
Why you had to die
And the other leaders
Will disappear
Today is the day you die.

LONG SEASON

Some of the trees are bare
The leaves flown south for the winter
Abandoning their maker.
Not aware they are dead
A few will make it.

It's when winter comes
That I remember and confirm
I was meant to be a bear
Let me hibernate
And wake up hungry

I am surrounded by those
Who profess to love this.
They drill holes in the ice
Looking for piscatorial gold
They smell like what they find.

This goes on forever
Like basketball and hockey
Me, I look for signs of life
Baseball, perhaps
Or golf in Hawaii.

Eventually the leaves come back
All svelte and green
The trees fill out
With a happy bushiness
And all is well.

By the time there was a knock on the door a couple of days later, Rita was no longer surprised. It was a young state trooper at the door to let her know Cliff had been found dead in his pickup about ten miles west of town on an abandoned farmstead. He had chosen asphyxiation. Apparently he had gone to the hardware store for some hose and duct tape.

Later, it was found out he had also made some purchases at the drugstore. The last person who saw him was the postal agent who remembered weighing and applying postage to the package he brought in. He said he noticed Cliff was moving very slowly as if in some pain.

The undertaker, in a private aside to Rita, asked about the mutilation but didn't pursue it beyond their brief conversation.

Her grief, which had started before she even knew he was dead, grew in days following the funeral. Sam called most days. The guilt she felt was unbearable.

About a week later, after not being able to reach her by phone, Sam stopped by.

As he walked through the house looking for her, he couldn't help but notice the messy household. It was so unlike his mother. A thorough search of the house did not produce his mother.

"Maybe she's in the barn" he decided and went to look for her there.

As he passed the garage an intuition caused him to stop. He thought he heard her car running softly in the background.

He became frightened and ran to the garage as quickly as he could.

Inside he found his mother slumped over in the front seat with the car running. She had chosen the same route as her husband.

Rita had left a note in the front seat with her. In it she asked forgiveness from God, Sam, and everyone. She had decided she must share Clifford's last pain and hoped with all her heart that if they met in Heaven he would forgive her.

DAVID'S ROSE

She was a star
Upon the bar
Doing all kinds
Of bumps and grinds
And going way too far

Or, so it seemed to me
Cuz' I could plainly see
Things my mommy said
I had better left unread
But then, I always welcome opportunity

To enjoy the art
Of a sassy little tart
Defying morals and
Bible-preaching pious man
Who just happened to be present at the start

Of this interesting show
To us hornies down below
The bar with stiff, sore necks
Our posture it did wreck
While the business in the booths began to grow.

Then, someone hollered "More!"
But, from my view in the store
It would be my gifted guess
What they got was even less
In the way of clothes as they fell to the floor.

THE NEW OLD ME

I died this morning and, for some, it was a loss.
I didn't get permission—not even from my boss.

And when I got to Heaven, all my teeth were there
And, better yet, to greet me, was all my missing hair!

My appendix came to say "Hello" and showed me right on in.
My missing sense of humor showed and gave to me a grin.

My memory came to welcome me (if I remember right).
And my high-school weight came back—I guess I once was light.

PHASES

When I first became aware
Of who I was
And who I wasn't
At that time it was, for me
A problem of scale.

When I was at that age
Where boys hate girls
Secretly, I liked you.
Without understanding why
I wanted to be with you.

When I began to change
Into a man
I noticed, of course
You were changing too
But you still let me like you.

When I became a man
Full of myself
Prideful, cocksure, insolent
Your patience and softness
Carried the day.

Today you are still here
Beside me, loving me
Your prayers have won out
Your faith rewarded
I am yours always.

TEEN TOWN
(FOR A DECEASED FRIEND)

Boys:
I'm not a good dancer
And there is no ball to catch.
What if I smell bad
Or, step on her toes
Or, she won't dance with me?

Girls:
There they are
Lined up against a wall
Are we the firing squad?
That one is cute
Think his name is Dave.

Boys:
I suppose we make the move
Am I zipped up?
"Oh, God! I'm nervous!"
I forget the steps
Hope the songs are slow.

Girls:
Here they come
Away from their wall
Towards ours
Like an advancing enemy
Bent on conquest.

Boys:
This one is pretty
She'll never dance with me
I'll ask someone else
And hope to be rejected?
What if she says "Yes.?"

Girls:

This one is shy
But dances okay
He doesn't talk
Probably concentrating
To make a good impression.

Boys:

Is the song almost over?
So far, so good
I think
How tight do I hold her?
Hey, this feels nice.

Girls:

Oh No—The song is over!
He did pretty good.
I must tell him
When I thank him.
Hope he asks again.

Widower's Walk

I wasn't ready for you to go.
So much to do and see.
I hadn't finished telling you
How much you meant to me.

Now all the plans I had for us
And the life we shared as one
Are up in smoke—there is no "us."
I can't believe it's done.

You always let me lead the way
With a gentle nudge or two
I always had the feeling that
The leader was really you.

Who's going to nudge me sweetly now?
Who's going to hold my hand?
Who's going to pray with me at night
I'm not a one-man band.

I fix my meals to eat as one.
I make the bed alone.
I clean the house. I do the chores.
My spirit's turned to stone.

I walk the Widower's Walk as one
I look for signs of God
I bide my time 'til I am called
To leave this Earthly sod.

PINE BOX OPUS

I have unlimited long-distance
So put my phone inside my coffin.
When I get to where I'm going
I will try to call you often.

If I see someone that knows us
And we did not owe them money
We will have a conversation
We will share some jokes quite funny.

We will comment on the weather
As if still in Minnesota.
Will the Vikings beat the Packers.
Will the Gophs lose to Dakota.

I will tell you of our kinfolk
Naming those who didn't arrive.
You will tell me what's a cooking
And what friends are still alive

As I lay there in my coffin
Trying all my apps to run
The question of the hour
Am I having any fun?

CONSTRUCTION ZONE

I am nothing
Only my own memory
Not even yours.
I am trying to rebuild
A thing that was never there
For you.

Each day, the dream's more vivid
Each night, the passion grows.
How can we be so far apart
You have forgotten me completely
I have etched you into my brain
I knew you had to be.

I try to build the memory up
To share in what I had
To make it what we had
Sometimes I think it's working
And at others, I see a wall
I think you're trying though.

I will prevail
I will not stop
The prize too great to lose
I must press on
But for now
I am nothing.

CHAR

She says "We're history."

I suggest "Burnt toast."

She says "What's the difference?"

I say "I don't throw burnt toast away."

She says "I do."

I say "No. You don't. You never throw anything away."

She says "I've changed."

I say "So have I."

She says "What makes toast burn?"

I say "Maybe the fire was too hot."

She says "Maybe it was in the toaster too long."

I say "Maybe."

She says "Even if you scrape away the burnt part, the toast will be cold by then.

I say "We could reheat it."

She says "We could burn it again."

I say "Maybe."

My Continental Divide

I don't know when, exactly, I lost my immortality.
But, recently, I realized I will die.
It was not a scary thought. I am tired.
I have achieved (or not) what I had hoped.

There I was. Sailing along.
Blissfully unaware of my own demise.
Even after my heart attack
It never occurred to me I could die!

I have become comfortable with God.
And I'm okay using his plan instead of mine.
Mine seemed to be complicated and full of traps.
His seems simple yet exquisite.

I'm also comfortable with God's decision.
When the time comes, do I go up or down?
I thank Him for my life—and I will say
Acepto.

GYPSY FREE
(HOMAGE TO JAMIE FARR'S CHARACTER, "ZOLTON")
(SHABOOM!)

You will not find us listed at the Halls of Deaths and Births
No tax man lives who knows how much our net is really worth
The census taker missed us as we were on the go
We have no babies that the local truant man can show
We weave in and out of peoples lives—they never really see
We're here today and then we're there, we're moving gypsy free

For centuries we've been brothers to the whims of fickle wind
We're always gone before we've made an enemy or friend
The Earth is our home, the river our bath, our roof is open sky
We claim joy our own treasure, you've never seen a gypsy cry
Our lives are ours, with woes behind like fish upon the sea
Our minds are clear, we ne'er regret, we're thinking gypsy free.

Would you like your palm read? Fortune rendered? A cure for any ail?
We guarantee our product or a refund without fail
Of course, you will not find us, we'll have hit the trail of dust
With a business mien like ours, anonymity is a must
But we'll be thinking of you as we're sure you'll think of we.
Perhaps with heartfelt longing to be also gypsy free.

MAIN PROGRAM

C:\Windows

Click on "Life"

  View the Tabula Rasa

  Select "Childhood"

      Run

      Create

      Draw

      Pause

      Reduce Childhood to Background

  Select "Adulthood"

      Edit

           Relationships

           Beliefs

           Values

           Expectations

      Merge

           Create Sub-files

      Save

  Select "Middle Age"

      Sort

      Delete

      Cut and Paste

      Save

      Drag

           Open "What if?"

              View "Options"

           View "Childhood" again

Close "Middle Age"

Close "Childhood"

Select "Maturity"

       Search for God

       Save

       Save

       Save

       Review Database

       Begin Distribution of Icons

       Find God

Close "Maturity"

Close "Adulthood"

Close "Life"

Close "Windows"

NEEDS MUSIC

ONLY SORRY

I think back upon our marriage years
And all the lies I bought.
This time it's just not working.
You're only sorry you got caught.

We had a fifty fifty marriage
At least, that's how we described the game.
It was always you took the credit
While giving me the blame.

Your phony contrition will get you no pass.
You're running in place and losing ground.
One foot on the brake and one on the gas
Your house of straw has just burned down.

Those times are now behind us dear
But they weren't lived for naught.
There's an air of freedom now to know
You're only sorry you got caught.

Your phony contrition will get you no pass.
You're running in place and losing ground.
One foot on the brake and one on the gas
Your house of straw has just burned down.

DOUBLE FEATURE

How many movies did you pay to see
A mere gratuity
For the use of the bumpy parking lot
With speakers on the tree?

How many movies did you joyfully miss
For the stolen kiss
The higher thrills and goose-bump chills
That could lead to all-night bliss?

The Starlight is a fading sight with weekend gigs into the night
Movies, now, are quite a fright
From PG to X and substance to sex
You have one chance to get it right.

How may times did you go to that video land with furrowed row
With no intention to view the show
To drink a beer with friends held dear
And forget one night your cares and woe.

The Starlight is a fading sight with weekend gigs into the night
Movies, now, are quite a fright
From PG to X and substance to sex
You have one chance to get it right.

New National Anthem (Proposed)
(To be sung to the tune of whatever works)

O say can you bail?
We are too big to fail.
Our cars are all junkers
Made perfect for clunkers.

Embrace the illegals
With nice gifts from Speigels
While our mismanaged banks
Only owe you their thanks

All our money they'll take
With a ninety percent rake.
For bonuses galore
Like a financial whore

"But we'll lose all that talent
If they don't get their pay."
No sillier argument is
Presented today.

Where would they go?
What would they do on the loose?
For that kind of money
There's only one golden goose.

Insure me, dear Gov.
And make me take shots.
Manage my life
Through the nursing home cots.

Pay for my funeral
Pay all my bills
School all my children
Cure all their ills.

Whence cometh all this money?
Where's the big money store?
Here's our new motto:
"We'll print more! We'll print more!"

THE THREE RS

Your note this morning said you won't
be coming back.
You had to satisfy some need.
As I read this many times I find
I wish I'd never learned to read.

As I write this page my thoughts
Go back to our first night
Each line here hurts a lot
I wish I'd never learned to write

Reading, 'riting, and romance
Three basics a young man learns.
Three skills are reinforced with
Each passing grade he earns.

Tonight, I'll be alone again
Like the single moon above.
Who waits forever for his turn
I wish I'd never learned of love.

WOULDN'T HEART

Try as I might and put up the fight
Oh, tell me, why did I even start?
The cupboard is bare, there's no loving there
I have the will but, you have a wouldn't heart.

Some think I'm crazy, others, you're lazy
Unwilling to play a part
But you lead me on with kisses and song
Throw me slivers of your wouldn't heart

How does it beat? How can it compete
With the real thing I wish to impart
My heart is for real. So let's make a deal
And put love in your once wouldn't heart.

HAVE YOU EVER?

Have you ever wakened from a dream so real your eyes were crying?
Have you ever been hurt by a hurt so bad you wish that you were dying?
Have you ever been told a truth so hard you wish that they were lying?

I've had the dream, I've felt the pain
I've heard the truth—again, again.

A dream that leaves you crying has come close upon your heart.
A hurt that wants you dying shouldn't have happened from the start.
A truth as hard as this can make your senses come apart.

I've had the dream, I've felt the pain
I've heard the truth—again, again.

I trade the dream for a peaceful night—for nocturnal, sleepy bliss
I forgive the hurt for one kind act, perhaps a stolen kiss
I own the truth with firm resolve to make amends for this

About the Author

Rudyard Thurber is, of course, an alias. In choosing a pseudonym, I was confronted by the fact that most of the good ones have been taken— Mark Twain, George Eliot, William Shakespeare, etc.. (Well, some people do think Shakespeare was really Francis Bacon.)

I chose this name because I really like Kipling's writing even though he seemed to have indifference toward women and I liked Thurber because he tried to explain them. It is true that, for the most part, he only proved that there are some things that should never be explained, just enjoyed and appreciated for their mystery.

This journey, then, is really a Mittyesque foray into the unknown. While his world was, in his own mind, a secret, in reality, today it is very difficult to keep secrets.

So, here then, I give you some of my secrets.

The author lives alone with his wife and children in St. Paul, Minnesota.

www.ingramcontent.com/pod-product-compliance
Lightning Source LLC
Chambersburg PA
CBHW031241260626
47169CB00007B/2395